Fairy Bears
Dizzy

"I promise to do my best. I promise to work hard to care for the world and all its plants, animals and children. This is the Fairy Bear Promise."

CANCELLED

Look out for more magical Fairy Bears!

Dizzy

Sunny

Blossom

Sparkle

Primrose

Misty

Lulu

Poppy

Visit the secret world of the Fairy Bears and explore the magical Crystal Caves . . .

www.fairybearsworld.com

Fairy Bears

Dizzy

Julie Sykes

Illustrated by Samantha Chaffey

MACMILLAN CHILDREN'S BOOKS

First published 2010 by Macmillan Children's Books
a division of Macmillan Publishers Limited
20 New Wharf Road, London N1 9RR
Basingstoke and Oxford
Associated companies throughout the world
www.panmacmillan.com

ISBN 978-0-330-51201-5

1 3 5 7 9 8 6 4 2

A CIP catalogue record for this book is available from
the British Library.

Printed and bound in the UK by CPI Mackays, Chatham ME5 8TD

For Antonia Louise MacPhee

Prologue

At the bottom of Firefly Meadow, not far from the stream, stands a tall sycamore tree. The tree is old with a thick grey trunk and spreading branches. Hidden amongst the branches is a forgotten squirrel hole. If you could fly through the squirrel hole and down the inside of the tree's hollow trunk, you would find a secret door that leads to a special place. Open the door and step inside the magical Crystal Caves, home of the Fairy Bears.

The Fairy Bears are always busy. They work hard caring for nature and children everywhere. You'll have to be quick to see them, and you'll have to believe in magic.

Fairy Bears

Do you believe in Fairy Bear magic?
Can you keep a secret? Then come on in –
the Fairy Bears would love to meet you.

Chapter One

"We're nearly there," said Dizzy the Fairy Bear, her stomach fluttering as she flew along the jewel-studded tunnel towards the school caves.

"Oh!" squeaked Sunny. "I'm not sure I'm ready for this."

"I am." Dizzy's brown eyes shone with excitement. "It's about time we were allowed to go out on our first task. We're not little cubs any more."

Dizzy flew faster, turning into the entrance of the school caves as the bell

sounded. Landing together, she and Sunny hurried across the playground to their class cave and went inside. Their teacher, Miss Alaska, hadn't arrived and the noise was deafening as all the Fairy Bears chattered at once. Minutes later Miss Alaska fluttered into the room carrying a huge pile of sycamore leaves. She put them on her stone desk then faced the class, her yellow-and-pink wings flapping impatiently as she waited for everyone to stop talking. One by one the Fairy Bears fell silent and sat up straight on their stone seats.

"Good morning, everyone," said Miss

Alaska, smiling warmly. "As you know, it's time to start going outside into the world to complete tasks. Each task will involve helping a person or an animal to overcome a problem. The tasks are really important. You have to pass them all to be able to move up into the senior class. If you fail a task, then you'll have to spend another year in the juniors with me. The tasks are written on these sycamore leaves. Only one Fairy Bear will go out on a task at a time. Are there any questions?"

Dizzy took a deep breath, forcing herself to sit still and not wiggle her lilac wings. This was the most exciting day of her life. Closing her eyes, she whispered, "Please let it be me."

"Good," said Miss Alaska, when no one raised a paw to ask a question. "Let's say the Fairy Bear Promise, and then we can begin."

Fairy Bears

Dizzy laid her wand on her desk then stood up with her wings neatly folded behind her. Holding paws with Sunny and Blossom, she began to chant with everyone else: "I promise to do my best. I promise to work hard to care for the world and all its plants, animals and children. This is the Fairy Bear Promise."

Dizzy gave Sunny's paw a little squeeze and Sunny squeezed her paw back. Miss Alaska reached for a sycamore leaf. Dizzy held her breath.

"The Fairy Bear going out on this first task is . . ." said Miss

6

Dizzy Dives In

Alaska, pausing dramatically, "Dizzy."

"Me!" spluttered Dizzy, nearly falling over her stone desk with excitement. She turned to Sunny and hugged her tightly. "Bouncing bears! Wish me luck, Sunny."

Grabbing her wand, Dizzy headed for the door.

"Not so fast, Dizzy," called Miss Alaska. "I haven't given you your task yet."

"Fluff brain," muttered Coral, a pretty white bear with blue eyes and pinky-orange wings.

Dizzy pretended not to hear. It was the best way to deal with Coral's nasty comments. Sunny gave an indignant growl.

"Just because her mum and dad work for the king and queen she thinks she's better than us, when really *she's* the fluff brain."

Dizzy laughed then quickly fell silent as Miss Alaska glared at her.

"I hope you're going to take this first task seriously, Dizzy," said Miss Alaska sternly.

"I am," Dizzy replied.

Miss Alaska stared at her for a moment longer then smiled.

"Good. Here it is then. You've got a very special job to do."

With trembling paws, Dizzy took the leaf and read it.

"I have to visit a girl called Louise and sprinkle her with good-luck magic," she said. "Louise is playing a recorder solo in her school's spring concert, but she's very nervous. She's scared she's going to make a mistake and ruin the show."

"That's a lovely task," said Sunny enviously. "Good luck, Dizzy."

"Good luck," called everyone except Coral, who rolled her eyes and gave a bored sigh.

Dizzy Dives In

"There's a map of Louise's house on the leaf," said Miss Alaska. "Before you leave, check that you know where you're going and that your wand is working properly."

Dizzy picked up her wand and stroked it lovingly. It had been a gift from her grandmother and was very special. The gold wand complemented Dizzy's pale gold fur. The purple, heart-shaped amethyst set in the star at its tip matched her lilac wings and eartips. Dizzy's wand was very reliable. It had never let her down before, but she couldn't resist sneaking a look in the magic mirror hung on the classroom wall for a little extra help.

Each class had a
magic mirror and
looking at one
was like looking
through a
window. You
never knew
what you
might see, but
often the mirror
showed you something useful. At first, as
Dizzy stared into the rectangular-shaped
glass edged with tiny crystals, a pretty bear
with lilac markings stared back.

"Please let me succeed," she whispered.

At once her reflection disappeared and in
its place Dizzy saw a young girl with long
blonde hair and green eyes. The girl's face
was tight with worry as she put a recorder
to her lips. Dizzy shivered. She hated

seeing a child look so anxious. The picture disappeared and Dizzy vowed to find Louise quickly and help her. Experimentally she waved her wand to check it was working properly. A stream of lilac stars whizzed from it in a perfect horseshoe shape, making the class giggle.

"That seems to be working fine," said Miss Alaska. "Off you go. Good luck, Dizzy. I know you won't let me down."

Dizzy's stomach gave a nervous growl as she left the classroom and headed for the Grand Door. This was it! Her task had started. It was time to leave the Crystal Caves and find Louise.

Chapter Two

Leaving the school behind her, Dizzy
turned into the long tunnel that led to the
Grand Door, the main way in and out of
the Crystal Caves. There was a stream of
Fairy Bears heading out for the day. Dizzy
joined them, her wings fluttering excitedly
as she hurried along. The tunnel walls
glowed softly, lit by thousands of jewels. It
was magic that made the jewels shine in
the dark and Dizzy rubbed a paw along the
wall, touching as many jewels as she could
in the hope that the magic would bring her

luck. Soon she passed the diamond arch marking the entrance to the Royal Caves. Dizzy stared in wonder. She'd seen the Fairy Bear king and queen once before at the midsummer ball and it was something she'd never forgotten. Queen Tania, with her rainbow-coloured wings, was the prettiest Fairy Bear in the world.

Nearing the end of the Main Tunnel, Dizzy caught a glimpse of the gnarled root staircase. There was a crowd of Fairy Bears waiting at the bottom. Dizzy joined the throng, inching forward until it was her turn and she could climb the wooden stairs to the Grand Door. The door was held open, but Dizzy ran her paw across

the leaf-shaped handle, loving the intricate carvings that made it look so real. She hesitated, then taking a deep breath to calm her nervous excitement she stepped through the door and into the hollow trunk of the sycamore tree. It was pitch black.

Dizzy stood for a moment to let her eyes adjust, her pale gold fur crackling with excitement. One of the best things about being inside the sycamore tree's thick trunk was the dark. Like all bears, Dizzy loved the dark and the way it wrapped around her like a soft, velvety blanket.

Fluttering her wings, Dizzy began her journey up the tree trunk. A stream of Fairy Bears flew up the tree's insides and the air sang with the hum of their wings. Dizzy had never travelled in the rush hour before and thought it was very exciting to be flying with so many other bears.

When she was halfway up the tree, the darkness was suddenly broken by a pale circle of light shining through the squirrel hole at the top of the trunk. Dizzy flew faster, eager to be on her way. She was in such a rush that she didn't notice the queue of Fairy Bears all waiting to fly through the squirrel hole until it was almost too late. She screeched to a halt, paws out to save herself from crashing, her wings frantically beating the air.

"Grrr," snapped an elderly bear with silvery wings as Dizzy accidentally jabbed him on the bottom with her outstretched wand. "Watch out, young bear. You'll hurt someone, poking at them like that."

"Sorry," Dizzy apologized.

She checked to see that her wand hadn't been damaged, but it was fine. Holding the wand tightly in her paw, Dizzy waited

quietly in the queue, hovering a safe distance
behind the bear in case he told her off again.

At last it was her turn. Dizzy dived
through the squirrel hole, blinking as she
came out into the bright morning sun.

"Hi, Dizzy."

Dizzy looked up and saw a chocolate-
coloured bear with light-green wings sitting
on the branch above her.

"Racer!" she called
in delight.

Racer was
in Mrs Pan's
class, and a
senior, but
they lived
near each
other and
were good
friends.

"What are you doing out by yourself?" Racer asked.

Dizzy puffed out her chest. "I'm doing my first task," she said proudly.

"How exciting!" said Racer, patting the branch he was sitting on with a paw. "Come and sit up here with me. You'll find your task much easier if you've thought about it carefully first. What have you got to do?"

Dizzy looked longingly at the branch. Racer was a lively bear with a good sense of humour. It would be fun to sit and chat with him. It might even calm the fizzy feeling in her tummy. Then, as she remembered Louise's anxious face, her wings twitched impatiently. There wasn't time to sit around. She had to go. Louise needed her help now.

"Next time," she called. "I'm in a hurry. I've got to sprinkle a girl with good-luck magic before she plays a recorder solo in her school concert."

Racer's green eyes twinkled and he saluted Dizzy with a chocolate-brown paw.

"That sounds urgent. Good luck."

"Thanks!" said Dizzy. She glanced at the map on her leaf. From Firefly Meadow she'd have to fly over the stream, across the fields to the village and on to the river. Then it was a right-wing turn, flying straight ahead to the train line, which, with another right-wing turn, she could follow until she reached Louise's village. It was a long way from the Crystal Caves, but it was an easy journey.

"Bouncing bears!" squeaked Dizzy, somersaulting in delight. Then, remembering she had an important job to do, she stopped her somersaults and wrapped the leaf round her wand for safe keeping.

It was a perfect spring morning. The sun was bright and the sky blue, with only a small cluster of clouds in the distance. Dizzy flew over the flower-filled meadow and across the stream. She flew quickly, anxious to find Louise and help her. At the grassy field Dizzy called out a hello to her friends the cows. The cows mooed back as Dizzy sped past.

A long time later, Dizzy slowed down. Her wings were beginning to ache. She should have reached the river by now, but all she could see was a dark smudge in the distance that looked like a town. Dizzy tried to remember the map. She didn't recall seeing a town on it. Puzzled, she flew down and perched on a thick hedge. She unrolled the sycamore leaf, tapping it with her wand to magically smooth out the wrinkles.

There was definitely no town marked on this map. Confused, Dizzy stared at the leaf. Where was she?

Oh no! Dizzy flapped her wings in annoyance. How could she have made such a silly mistake? In her hurry to start her task, she'd been looking at the map upside down and flown in completely the wrong direction. Dizzy's heart thumped uncomfortably. If only she'd taken Racer's advice and sat with him in the tree to get her thoughts together. Poor Louise! She should be with her by now.

Remembering Louise's pinched face made Dizzy feel awful. If she failed her task, Dizzy wouldn't be the only one to suffer. Louise would too!

Chapter Three

With trembling paws, Dizzy wrapped the leaf back round her wand.

"Honey mites!" she growled crossly as she couldn't get the leaf to lie flat and had to unroll it and start again.

There was much more traffic in the air as Dizzy retraced her earlier flight. She had to concentrate on where she was going to avoid a collision. She passed butterflies, a lacewing, several flies and two ladybirds. They all seemed in a hurry too, just like Dizzy. Holding her wand tightly, Dizzy continued her journey, following the railway line until she spotted Louise's village.

"Bouncing bears!" exclaimed Dizzy, relieved that she was nearly there. She'd been flying for so long her wings were aching.

Louise's house was on the village outskirts backing on to fields. As Dizzy flew towards it, her ears began to twitch. What was that? Dizzy's paws tingled with excitement at the pretty music. Swiftly she followed it to the back of the house. The music was floating through an upstairs window. Dizzy peeked inside and saw a slim girl with long blonde hair playing a recorder. Her eyes were screwed up in concentration as she worked at getting the right notes.

"Louise," whispered Dizzy softly.

Filled with excitement, she dipped down

and flew through the open window into
the bedroom. It was the first time Dizzy
had been inside a human house and for
a minute her curiosity got the better of
her. Louise's room was wonderful, with a
gorgeous lilac duvet that matched Dizzy's
wings exactly, and silver stars on the
ceiling! There was a bookcase crammed
with books and a tall wardrobe covered
with pictures of animals. Louise's school

bag, leaning against her dressing table, had animals on it too. Louise was playing from a sheet of music propped on a stand.

Dizzy's eyes widened at the enormous piece of paper. The musical notes written there were nearly as high as she was. Dizzy enjoyed music at school and was especially good at Fairy Bear flute. But there was something wrong here. The notes on Louise's sheet of music weren't moving. No wonder Louise was nervous. How could she follow the tune if the notes on the page stayed flat and lifeless?

"Bouncing bears!" Dizzy exclaimed.

Impulsively she swooped towards the paper, meaning to fix the notes, but as she raised her wand everything went black. Surprised, Dizzy hovered while her eyes adjusted to the dark. Her wings brushed against something soft, yet solid as a wall.

Dizzy Dives In

Dizzy turned but the soft solid thing was all around her, trapping her. Dizzy's wings beat frantically. She was so scared she could hardly breathe. She'd been careless and now she was trapped. Her paws were shaking. She wondered if she was in any danger. Then suddenly her prison walls began to tremble and Dizzy heard an amazing noise. It reminded her of sunshine and waterfalls.

"Oooh, that tickles," giggled a voice.

A gap appeared in Dizzy's prison and a green eye stared at her.

"A fairy," breathed Louise softly. "Or are you a bear?"

Suddenly the walls opened up and Dizzy realized she was sitting in the palm of Louise's hand. They stared at each other for a moment then Dizzy said, "I'm a Fairy Bear."

"A Fairy Bear! What's that?"

"Me," said Dizzy, proudly puffing out her pale gold chest. "Fairy Bears are descended from the great bear Ursa  Major. A long time ago, Ursa Major found a fairy with injured wings and he carried her safely home. Many years later, the fairy was able to pay him back. Ursa Major was being chased by hunters and the fairy turned him into a Fairy Bear so he could escape."

"That's a lovely story!" exclaimed Louise. "So are Fairy Bears like real fairies? Can they do magic too?"

"Yes," said Dizzy, nodding. "We mostly use our magic to look after the world and all its living things."

Louise stared at Dizzy as if she could hardly believe her eyes.

"What's your name?" she asked at last.

"Dizzy. You play the recorder really nicely," Dizzy added shyly.

"Do I?" Louise was surprised but pleased. "I'm playing a solo in the school spring concert tomorrow. Mum and Dad are coming and so are Grandma and Grandad. I'm really nervous. What if I mess it up?"

"You won't mess it up once I've fixed your notes for you," said Dizzy. "I was about to mend them when you caught me."

"Fix my notes?" Louise sounded puzzled.

"Yes," said Dizzy, flying out of Louise's hand and landing on the sheet of music. "They're not moving."

"They're not supposed to move." Louise's eyes suddenly widened. "Do your notes move, then?"

"Yes, they dance the music so we know what to play," Dizzy explained.

Louise giggled, making Dizzy giggle too.

"That's so cool." She put her recorder on the bed and sat cross-legged next to it. "Tell me about your home."

"Tell me about the concert first," said Dizzy. "Why are you nervous about making a mistake? You play really well."

"That's just it," said Louise slowly, kneading the duvet with her fingers. "I'm fine when I'm playing for fun, but when people are watching me my brain sort of freezes up. Then I can't remember where

to put my fingers to make the notes.
It happened last week when we were
practising at school and Jenna – she's this
really horrible girl in my class – laughed
and called me stupid."

"She sounds like Coral," said Dizzy
sympathetically. "She's a Fairy Bear in
my class and she calls me fluff brain. You
should ignore her. It works on Coral."

"I do most of the time," sighed Louise.
"But knowing that Jenna is waiting for
me to make a mistake is making me so
nervous. Grandma and Grandad are
visiting especially to hear me play. I want
to do well in the concert for them."

Dizzy's fur crackled with excitement.
Should she tell Louise about the good-luck
magic? Or would it be better to secretly
sprinkle her with it before she left? She
hadn't thought to ask what to do if she was

spotted by a human. What if she did the wrong thing and failed the task?

"Will you play for me again?" she asked, deciding not to tell Louise about the good-luck stars just yet.

Louise's cheeks turned pink.

"OK," she said. "I'll imagine I'm playing at the concert. Maybe that will help to cure my nerves."

Picking up her recorder, she slid off the bed and stood in front of the music stand. With her free hand she flicked her hair over her shoulder. Then she took a deep breath.

"Welcome to Barleyfield Primary School's spring concert," she said grandly. "We start with Louise Shaw playing Beethoven's 'Ode to Joy' on her recorder." Louise paused then added, "Beethoven's the composer. He wrote the music."

Louise lifted the recorder to her lips and

played the opening notes. Dizzy, who was still sitting on the sheet of music, got blasted with air and toppled backwards.

"Help!" she cried.

Her lilac wings fluttered frantically as she struggled to right herself.

The music stopped abruptly as Louise leaped forward to catch Dizzy.

"I'm sorry," she squeaked.

Dizzy landed lightly in the palm of Louise's hand.

"Don't be upset. It was my fault for sitting there." Dizzy burst out laughing and after a second Louise laughed too.

"You gave me such a fright," she said. "I thought I'd hurt you."

"Louise?"

33

Footsteps sounded outside and the bedroom door swung open. Mrs Shaw stared at her daughter in surprise. "Is everything all right? I thought I heard you talking to someone."

"E-er," stuttered Louise. "I was practising for the concert tomorrow."

"Darling," said Mrs Shaw, sweeping across the room with outstretched arms to hug her daughter. "You're not still worrying about it, are you? You'll be fine. It's almost tea time. Put your recorder away and go and wash your hands."

Dizzy Dives In

Thinking that she might get crushed, Dizzy swooped into the air.

"A bee!" exclaimed Mrs Shaw. "Stand still, darling. They only sting if they think they're in danger."

She snatched Louise's music from the stand and swatted at Dizzy.

"Eeek!" growled Dizzy, darting out of the way.

"Oh no you don't!" said Mrs Shaw, leaping across the room and kicking the door shut. "It's out of the window for you."

That's where I'm trying to go, thought a terrified Dizzy, buzzing away.

"Out!" shouted Mrs Shaw, flapping at Dizzy with the paper again.

"Don't hurt her!" cried Louise.

Dizzy's heart was beating so hard she thought it might explode. She dived towards the window. Mrs Shaw was close behind. Dizzy could feel the paper coming closer, but she didn't dare look back. Would she get swatted this time? Her pale gold fur stood on end at the thought.

"Mum, NO!" yelled Louise, grabbing her mother by the arm and tugging her away. "You'll hurt her."

"I'm not trying to hurt it. I'm trying to help it out of the window," said Mrs Shaw, pausing to reassure Louise.

With an extra burst of speed, Dizzy sped towards the window and flew outside. Panting heavily, she collapsed on the window ledge as Mrs Shaw slammed the window shut behind her. Dizzy's wings trembled as she struggled to control her breathing. That had been awful! Mrs Shaw had almost hit her twice. Dizzy hadn't managed to sprinkle Louise with good-luck stars either. She peered through

the glass, wondering if Louise would let
her in when her mother had gone.
Louise's frightened face peered back at
her.

"Are you OK?" she mouthed.

"Yes," said Dizzy, wiggling her wings to
prove she was.

Louise looked relieved.

"Sorry," she said, close to the glass. "I
have to go now. It's tea time. Will you be
here when I've eaten?"

Suddenly Dizzy realized how late it
was getting. There wasn't time to wait for
Louise to finish her tea so she could sprinkle
her with good-luck magic. She'd fail her
task completely if she wasn't home before
nightfall.

"I have to go home, but I promise I'll be
back," she called, pressing her brown nose
against the glass and hoping Louise could

hear her. "I'll come tomorrow before your concert."

Mrs Shaw strode towards the window to see what Louise was looking at. With a hurried wave, Louise turned away.

Dizzy stared forlornly at Louise as she left the bedroom. Had she heard her promise? Vowing to return at first light the next day, Dizzy flew home.

Chapter Four

The scare in Louise's bedroom had worn
Dizzy out, but there was no time to rest.
Rallying herself, she flew home as fast as
she could. She had a long way to go and
after a while the light began to fade. Would
she get back in time? Dizzy forced her tired
wings to fly faster. She couldn't fail now
or she'd be letting Louise down too. At last
she reached Firefly Meadow. Down by the
stream the old sycamore tree welcomed her
home with outstretched branches. With a
last burst of speed, Dizzy dived between

its leaves and straight through the squirrel hole.

"I made it!" she cheered as she triumphantly coasted to the bottom of the hollow trunk.

Her relief at getting home was short-lived. Miss Alaska was waiting for her at the Grand Door.

"In the nick of time," she said, tapping her pen on the leaf pad she was holding. "Any later and you'd have failed for staying out in the dark."

She scribbled some notes on the leaf, then smiled at Dizzy expectantly.

"How did you get on?"

Dizzy tried to smile back, but couldn't. Her disappointment was too strong. She thought she'd be telling Miss Alaska that she'd completed her task.

"I found Louise, but didn't manage to

sprinkle her with good-luck stars," she whispered, staring at her paws.

Miss Alaska flicked back through her leaf pad.

"Hmmm," she said. "There's still time. The concert's tomorrow, isn't it? Do you want to try again?"

"Yes," said Dizzy emphatically. Not trying again hadn't even occurred to her.

"That's the spirit," said Miss Alaska, looking pleased. She ran a claw through her light-brown fur. "Maybe more thought and a little less speed tomorrow!"

Dizzy's face flamed. Miss Alaska gently touched one of Dizzy's lilac wings with her own yellow-and-pink one.

"Not many juniors complete their first task in a day," she said kindly. "Flutter along home now or your mum and dad will worry about where you've got to."

"Thanks," said Dizzy.

Dizzy hurried down the Main Tunnel, the colourful jewel-studded walls lighting the worn stone path. After a while, she turned off the main route, continuing past her school until the tunnel forked in two directions. There she hesitated. She really wanted to go and see Sunny and tell her about her disastrous day. They'd been best friends since they were little cubs and were always there for each other. Maybe Sunny could cheer Dizzy up. But as she stood deciding whether there was enough time she heard voices coming towards her.

"Thanks for inviting me to tea, Sunny. It was great fun," said Blossom.

"I had a good time too," answered Sunny.

Quickly Dizzy fluttered out of sight into the tunnel that led to her own cave. She

felt a little hurt that Sunny had been busy playing with Blossom. Had Sunny forgotten her already? Sighing sadly, Dizzy went home.

Mum and Dad were very excited that Dizzy had started her first task and wanted to hear all about it. After having her tea and answering all their questions, Dizzy managed to escape to her bedcave. She lay in her cosy bed but she couldn't sleep. Each time she closed her eyes she saw Sunny and Blossom laughing together. What if Sunny decided she liked Blossom better than Dizzy? She was scared she might lose her best friend.

The following morning Dizzy woke early with a horrible feeling inside her. Miserably she remembered how Sunny had gone off with Blossom. Dizzy rolled

out of bed, knocking her leaf duvet, filled
with moss, to the floor. She wouldn't
think about Sunny yet – today was about
Louise.

As she combed her fur, Dizzy conjured up
Louise's smiling face. How was she feeling?
Was she as nervous as Dizzy felt?

Mum and Dad had prepared a huge
breakfast. Dizzy was too anxious to eat
much, but she sipped nectar juice from her
stone mug and
dutifully nibbled on
a honey biscuit.

"Good
luck,"
said Mum
and Dad,
giving
her a
bear hug.

"Thanks," said Dizzy, determined to do her best.

As Dizzy approached the Grand Door, she heard someone call out her name. Turning round, she was surprised to see Sunny flying after her.

"Wait! Tell me about yesterday. I was desperate to know how you'd done. Why didn't you come and see me when you got back?"

"Erm . . ." said Dizzy, unable to fib to her friend. "I saw you with Blossom and felt I'd be in the way."

"Dizzy!" exclaimed Sunny. "Just because I was playing with Blossom doesn't mean I'd forgotten you. We're still best friends – but it's good to have other friends too."

Dizzy grinned, feeling foolish and happy at the same time. Of course it was good to have lots of friends. She'd made friends with Louise, hadn't she? Suddenly Dizzy felt much more confident about completing her task. All she had to do was fly back to Louise's house and sprinkle her with good-luck stars. What could be easier?

"This time I promise I'll come to see you when I get back," she said, lightly brushing her lilac wingtip against Sunny's yellow one. "Bye, Sunny."

Dizzy half flew, half ran up the gnarled root staircase to the Grand Door.

"I'll be waiting for you," Sunny called after her. "Good luck, Dizzy."

Sunny's good-luck wishes were so enthusiastic that Dizzy could still hear her calling out even when she was too far up the tree trunk to see her friend.

The early-morning air was chilly, making Dizzy's pale gold fur fluff out when she flew outside.

I look huge, like a grizzly bear, she thought happily.

Dizzy zipped along, her wings sparkling in the bright sunshine. She couldn't wait to see Louise again. Was she suffering from the same fluttery feeling Dizzy had? Had her brain frozen so that she couldn't remember how to play her recorder?

Dizzy was so concerned for Louise that she wasn't watching where she was going. An angry screech alerted her that something was in her way.
Snapping out of her daydream, Dizzy saw a brown-and-red butterfly heading towards her on a collision course.

"Bouncing bears,"

squeaked Dizzy, flying higher just as the
butterfly dipped lower. They passed each
other with millimetres to spare. The butterfly
glared at her angrily as it fluttered away.

Dizzy slowed down. Even her wings were
trembling at the fright she'd just had.

"More thought and less speed," Miss
Alaska had said. Suddenly Dizzy realized
how good that advice was.

At the river, Dizzy made a right-wing turn
and flew over the fields until she reached the
train line. Not far now! The fluttery feeling
in her stomach was almost unbearable.
What if Louise's bedroom window was shut?
Would Louise hear if she tapped on the
window? Nervously Dizzy flew on.

As she arrived, she saw that Louise's
bedroom window was wide open. Resisting
the urge to somersault for joy, she gracefully
swooped through it then stopped in mid-air.

Where was Louise? Her bed was neatly made and her bag was gone.

"No!" groaned Dizzy. Surely Louise hadn't left for school already?

Chapter Five

At that moment a familiar sound drifted
through the window. Dizzy settled on
the window ledge, her ears pricked and
her brown eyes hopeful. There was no
mistaking that joyful tune. It was Louise
playing her solo on the recorder. The music
was coming from the bottom of the garden.
Feeling relieved, Dizzy flew outside to find
her new friend.

Louise was standing with her back to
Dizzy, her blonde hair swinging gently as
her body moved in time with the music.

Dizzy hovered in the air to listen. How could Louise doubt herself when she played so beautifully?

Then, unexpectedly, the music faltered. Louise played a wrong note and, trying to correct it, blew too hard, making the recorder shriek in protest. Dizzy winced. All Louise needed to do was relax when she was playing.

Impulsively Dizzy dived towards her, determined to boost Louise's confidence with a shower of special good-luck stars. As she zoomed closer, she pointed her wand at Louise and called:

"Good luck to you
in all you do."

Magic rushed through the wand, making it glow with warmth. The heart-shaped amethyst twinkled brightly. With a soft hiss, a shower of tiny sparkling lilac stars suddenly burst from the wand. As they spun towards Louise, she missed two more notes, then suddenly stopped playing and leaned forward with a puzzled frown.

If Dizzy hadn't been in such a rush, the tumbling stars would have fallen over Louise, but her change of position meant that they missed. The stars landed on the grass beside her and fizzled away. One fell on a passing ant. The tiny creature paused for a moment, then jumped in the air, merrily kicking its legs as it scurried on.

"Brilliant!" said Dizzy bitterly. What a waste of magic!

Louise was on the move again. Leaving her recorder lying in the grass, she ran to the fence at the bottom of the garden.

Dizzy flew after her. "Louise," she called. "Wait for me."

She finally caught up when Louise stopped to open the garden gate.

"Dizzy!" Louise's face lit up. "I knew you'd come back."

Shyly she held out her hand and Dizzy gently coasted down to land in Louise's open palm.

"Where are you going? I thought the spring concert was today."

"It is," said Louise, pulling a face. "I woke early and couldn't get back to sleep thinking about it. I wanted more practice. I came outside so I wouldn't wake anyone. But I keep hearing a funny noise. Listen, there it is again."

Dizzy Dives In

Dizzy stood very still on Louise's palm and listened.

"It's a rabbit," she said at last. "It sounds hurt.'

"You're right!" exclaimed Louise. "It does sound like a rabbit squeaking."

She hurried through the gate and into the grassy field behind the house with Dizzy flying beside her.

"I bet the rabbit's in this field somewhere. I've seen loads of them out here." Her eyes raked over the grass.

Dizzy fluttered into the air and flew in a wide circle.

"Over there," she said, pointing with a paw.

Louise swung round and saw where she was pointing. The rabbit was tangled in a carrier bag and struggling like mad to free itself.

"It's only a baby!" Louise cried. "We have to help it before it gets hurt."

Taking slow steps and making gentle crooning noises, Louise headed towards the rabbit.

"We're here to help," she murmured soothingly. "We're your friends."

Dizzy whizzed towards the rabbit, raising her wand to perform a calming spell. But as she reached her the rabbit stopped struggling and sat with quivering ears, as if listening to Louise's voice. Dizzy lowered her wand. Louise had calmed the rabbit on her own.

The Fairy Bear hovered by her shoulder, watching as Louise slowly extended a hand. When the rabbit plucked up the courage to sniff at it, Louise stretched out a finger and gently stroked her on the head.

"We'll soon have you free," she whispered.

Dizzy Dives In

Dizzy had been itching to help the rabbit, but Louise's calm manner was having an effect on her too. She fluttered in the air, content to watch as Louise slowly gained the rabbit's trust. Soon the rabbit was so relaxed she looked like she might fall asleep. Then Louise began to work on untangling her from the carrier bag. It was more difficult than it looked. The plastic bag was tightly wrapped around the rabbit's whole body and Louise's slender fingers weren't strong enough to undo the knots.

"We need scissors," she said eventually.

"Here, let me try," said Dizzy.

Pleased to be helping, Dizzy flew closer. The rabbit's whiskers twitched. Her scared eyes begged Dizzy to free her from the plastic prison engulfing her tiny body. Dizzy flew down and settled on the rabbit's back. At first she wasn't sure where to start.

Then the rabbit shook her head as if to say, "Here." Dizzy reached forward, touched the rabbit's head with the tip of her wand and murmured:

> *"Magic, do your best for me,*
> *set this baby rabbit free."*

The wand hissed like a firework and suddenly became so warm that Dizzy almost dropped it. The heart-shaped amethyst glowed brightly as a fountain of lilac stars cascaded over the plastic bag and began melting it away.

"That's amazing," gasped Louise in delight.

Soon the rabbit's head and front paws were free. The rabbit licked them with a tiny pink tongue. Gratefully Dizzy rested on the rabbit's back. This was very strong magic and she felt tired. After a bit she scrambled up, ready to continue. Her wand felt lukewarm and spluttered when she waved it at the rabbit's back legs. Dizzy's forehead creased in a worried frown.

"Are you all right?" asked Louise.

"I'm fine," said Dizzy.

As she was about to try again, an awful thought struck her. Strong magic was hard work and needed lots of practice to do it well. What if she wore herself out helping the rabbit? She would need to rest before she was able to use her magic again to help Louise. But there wasn't time for a rest. Louise was playing in her concert very soon. Dizzy twiddled the wand in her paw. Should she continue to help the rabbit or save her magic for Louise?

Louise smiled encouragingly. She seemed very relaxed. It was as if she'd forgotten her concert nerves. Remembering all the hard work Louise had put into practising her recorder, Dizzy thought that she didn't really need her help.

I'll use my magic on the rabbit, she decided. Maybe she would still be able help Louise afterwards anyway.

Dizzy raised her wand, ready to continue, when another awful thought struck her. She *had* to give Louise some good-luck magic. If she didn't, then she would fail her first task and be forced to spend another year in the juniors. Dizzy groaned silently. What should she do?

The rabbit began to wriggle but her back legs were still tightly wrapped in plastic and she squeaked with fright. Suddenly Dizzy had the answer to her dilemma. Bravely she pointed her wand at the rabbit's legs as she murmured her spell:

"Magic, do your best for me,
set this baby rabbit free."

This time the wand hardly got warm at all.
A thin stream of lilac stars trickled from the
end and drifted over the rabbit. Dizzy held
her breath. Had she made enough magic
stars?

"It's working," gasped Louise. She
carefully pulled the melting plastic away
from the rabbit's hind legs. "You did it."

"Hooray!" cheered Dizzy. She was so
elated she leaped in the air and
turned a cartwheel.

Louise laughed.

"I wish I could
do that," she said
enviously.

Dizzy flopped on the
rabbit's back again.

Dizzy Dives In

"I wish I hadn't!" she groaned. "Now I'm completely worn out!"

Realizing she was now free, the rabbit nuzzled Louise's hand then quickly hopped away, sending Dizzy flying through the air.

"Help!" she cried.

In a flurry of wings, she righted herself and landed on Louise's nose. Giggling happily, Louise squinted at Dizzy with crossed eyes.

"I'm so glad I met you," she sighed. "This is the best day of my life."

"Mine too," said Dizzy, fluttering off Louise's nose and hovering in the air.

"Louise! Louise, where are you?"

Louise looked startled.

"That's Mum. Goodness, is that the time?" She stared at her watch in disbelief. "I have to go or I'm going to be late for the concert."

Chapter Six

"Wait!" cried Dizzy, suddenly remembering she hadn't even tried to sprinkle Louise with good-luck stars.

Louise was too far away to hear. Dizzy stared after her, pleased at how confident she seemed. She didn't need Dizzy's good-luck magic any more. But Dizzy wasn't prepared to fail her task without even trying. She flitted after her, catching up with Louise as she reached the back door. Mrs Shaw had already gone inside when Dizzy dived in front of Louise.

"Dizzy! You made me jump. What's up?"

"I've been trying to give you this," panted Dizzy, hoping she could summon the energy to bring Louise good luck.

Fluttering in the air on tired wings, she waved her wand and chanted:

"Good-luck stars are in order,
To help Louise play her recorder."

The wand spluttered like a spent firework. The heart-shaped amethyst glowed faintly, but no magic stars came out of the end.

"Honey mites!" groaned Dizzy in disappointment. "I was supposed to give you good-luck magic to help you play well in your concert, but helping the rabbit has worn me out. I'm going to need a rest before I can do any more strong magic. I'm sorry, Louise." Her lilac wings drooped.

"Don't be sad," said Louise, her eyes sparkling. "Meeting you and helping the rabbit has cured my nerves completely. Can you believe I'm actually looking forward to playing in the concert now? It's going to be brilliant. I bet even Jenna claps!"

"Hooray!" cheered Dizzy. She might have failed her first task, but at least she hadn't failed Louise. Joyfully, Dizzy turned a somersault.

Louise burst out laughing.

"I really wish I could do that," she said wistfully.

"Maybe one day I'll teach you," Dizzy answered, her wings quivering at the thought.

"Will you?" Louise stared at Dizzy, her mouth open. "Does that mean I might see you again?"

"I hope so," said Dizzy.

Suddenly she had a brilliant idea. She didn't have the energy for strong magic, but maybe she could do something simple. Waving her wand in a circle, she concentrated on a spell Miss Polar had taught her way back in cub class:

> *"From me to you,*
> *A star that's true."*

The wand juddered in Dizzy's paws, and with an enormous pop a single lilac star squeezed out of its tip. The star was so big that tiny Dizzy needed two paws to hand it to Louise.

"Keep this to remember me by," said Dizzy.

Louise took the star and held it in her

hand with a sigh of happiness.

"Thank you," she breathed.

"Louise," Mrs Shaw called from the kitchen. "Hurry up. It's time to go."

"Bye, Dizzy. I'll never forget you." Louise's fingers curled protectively round her friendship star.

"Bye, Louise," called Dizzy, soaring high in the air.

Dizzy was halfway home when the warm glow of happiness inside her began to fade. What was she going to say to Miss Alaska? Would her teacher be very cross that she'd used her magic to help a baby rabbit instead of Louise? And what would her parents say? Dizzy hoped they wouldn't be too disappointed in her. For once she didn't feel like flying fast. She held back, wishing her journey home could take forever.

Fairy Bears

Miss Brown had taken her class, the infants, out into Firefly Meadow to learn about wildflowers. Dizzy tried not to notice them as she flew towards the sycamore tree. At the end of the year, the infants would move up to Miss Alaska's class and become juniors. Dizzy had hoped she would move on too, becoming a senior in Mrs Pan's class. But that wasn't going to happen now. She'd failed her first task. She would be left behind in the juniors to repeat the year.

"Well, it's no good crying over spilt honey," said Dizzy, echoing one of her grandmother's sayings. Swallowing her disappointment, she flew through the branches of the sycamore tree and dived into the squirrel hole. Inside the tree, she hovered for a moment, enjoying the dark wrapping itself around her protectively.

"Here goes," Dizzy whispered.

Dizzy Dives In

Ready to face Miss Alaska, Dizzy flew down the inside of the tree trunk and entered the Crystal Caves through the Grand Door. She walked down the gnarled root staircase then flew along the deserted tunnels, arriving at the school caves far quicker than she wanted to. It was almost lunchtime and, smelling warm honey cakes, Dizzy's nose twitched. The school cook made delicious cakes, but Dizzy was too sad to feel hungry. She stepped into her classroom and the first Fairy Bear she saw was Coral, sitting at her desk, polishing her claws.

"Did you pass?" asked Coral in a bored voice.

Dizzy said nothing as she made her way to Miss Alaska's desk.

"You didn't, did you?" Coral's blue eyes widened. "You've failed your first task. What a fluff brain!"

The Fairy Bear giggled nastily. Dizzy's wings stiffened, but she kept her head high and carried on walking. Miss Alaska was busy collecting work, but when she saw Dizzy she stopped.

"You're back!" she exclaimed. "How did you get on?"

Dizzy shook her head, not trusting herself to speak. The class fell silent and Dizzy knew that everyone was looking at her.

Suddenly she was so nervous she could feel her wings knocking together.

"I failed," she whispered miserably. "I used all my magic up to help a rabbit."

In a low voice, Dizzy explained how she'd helped Louise to rescue the baby rabbit and then didn't have enough magical energy left to perform the good-luck spell on Louise. She stared at her paws, waiting for Miss Alaska to tell her off. But to her surprise Miss Alaska turned to the class and asked, "Has Dizzy made a good job of her task?"

"No," shouted Coral gleefully. "She's a fluff brain."

"Stop shouting, Coral. Put your paw up if you have something to say," said Miss Alaska sharply.

Sunny's paw was so high in the air she was nearly falling off her seat with the effort of keeping it there.

"Sunny, what do you think?"

"I think Dizzy did a very special thing," she said, smiling at her friend. "She put the baby rabbit before herself. Fairy Bears should always think of other creatures before themselves."

Miss Alaska clapped her paws together.

"Well done, Sunny. You're quite right. Fairy Bears must think of others before themselves. The baby rabbit would have been badly injured if Dizzy hadn't rescued her. And she did complete her task. Dizzy was clever enough to help Louise gain the confidence she needed to play her recorder without using magic."

For a moment the silence in the cave

was so deep it felt to Dizzy like everyone had gone into hibernation. Then the class erupted – clapping, cheering and wiggling their wings as they congratulated her. Only Coral, her face as sour as old milk, didn't join in.

Dizzy's pale gold fur flushed pink with pleasure. She had passed her first task! Mum and Dad would be so proud of her.

"Well done, Dizzy," said Miss Alaska, lightly tapping Dizzy's lilac wing with her own yellow-and-pink one. "You can have three honey-bee points."

"Thank you," gasped Dizzy. Honey-bee points were awarded for good work or good behaviour. When you'd filled a whole honey pot with honey-bee points, you could exchange it for a jar of real honey, Fairy Bears' favourite food.

The bell sounded for lunch and Dizzy

started for the door.

"Not so fast, Dizzy!" Miss Alaska laughed. "You've forgotten to collect your honey-bee points."

"Sorry," Dizzy apologized.

More thought, less speed, she remembered as she plopped the bee-shaped tokens into her jar. But she was too excited to take things slowly today, and there were honey cakes for lunch.

"Ready, Sunny?" she asked, grabbing her friend by the paw. "Come on then. I'm starving."

Fairy Bears Fact File

Dizzy

1. Favourite colour – *lilac*

2. Favourite gemstone – *amethyst*

3. Best flower – *knapweed*

4. Cutest animal – *tabby kitten*

5. Birthday month – *December*

6. Yummiest food – *honey cakes*

7. Favourite place – *Firefly Meadow*

8. Hobbies – *Fairy Bear flute, dancing*

9. Best ever season – *spring*

10. Worst thing – *having to sit still*

Your Fact File

━ ━ ━ ━ ━ ━ ━

1. Favourite colour – _ _ _ _ _ _ _

   2. Favourite gemstone – _ _ _ _ _ _ _ _

3. Best flower – _ _ _ _ _ _ _

   4. Cutest animal – _ _ _ _ _ _ _ _

5. Birthday month – _ _ _ _ _ _ _

   6. Yummiest food – _ _ _ _ _ _ _

7. Favourite place – _ _ _ _ _ _ _

   8. Hobbies – _ _ _ _ _ _ _

9. Best ever season – _ _ _ _ _ _ _

   10. Worst thing – _ _ _ _ _ _ _

Fairy Bears
Sunny

Sunny's Surprise

Friendly Fairy Bear Sunny sees Ella
looking sad in her magic mirror.
Sunny promises to cheer Ella up,
but how will she find her?

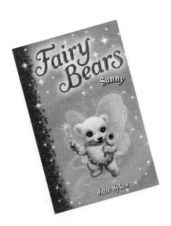

Fairy Bears
Blossom

Blossom the Brave

Bashful Blossom is determined
to cure Chloe of her stage fright.
But Blossom's magic won't work
unless she believes in herself first.

Fairy Bears

Sparkle

Sparkle Saves the Day

Sassy Sparkle loves pretty things.
Her task is to help a colony of
beautiful butterflies – but lonely
Isabel needs a sprinkling of Fairy
Bear magic too . . .

Fairy Bears

Primrose

A Puzzle for Primrose

Brainy Primrose is stuck!
Her task is to help a sad little
dog, but she keeps seeing Lucy in
the magic mirror. Will she solve
the puzzle in time?

Fairy Bears

Misty

Misty Makes Friends

Caring Misty must help Jessica
and her stepsister Becky to become
friends. But being confident isn't
easy for everyone . . .

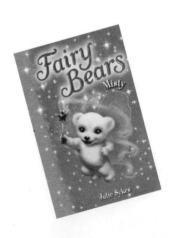

Collect tokens from each Fairy Bears book to WIN!

What prizes can you get?

- **tokens** get a Fairy Bears colour poster for your wall!
- **tokens** get a sheet of super-cute Fairy Bears stickers!
- **tokens** get a set of postcards to send to your friends, plus a certificate signed by the Fairy Bears creator, Julie Sykes!

Send them in as soon as you get them or wait and collect more for a bigger and better prize!

Send in the correct number of tokens, along with your name, address and parent/guardian's signature (you must get your parent/guardian's signature to take part in this offer) to: Fairy Bears Collection, Marketing Dept, Macmillan Children's Books, 20 New Wharf Road, London N1 9RR.

Fairy Bears Token Offer

1 Token
Prizes available while stocks last. See www.fairybearsworld.com for more details

Fairy Bears Token Offer

1 Token
Prizes available while stocks last. See www.fairybearsworld.com for more details

Fairy Bears

By Julie Sykes

Discover more friendly Fairy Bears!

Dizzy	978-0-330-51201-5	£3.99
Sunny	978-0-330-51202-2	£3.99
Blossom	978-0-330-51203-9	£3.99
Sparkle	978-0-330-51204-6	£3.99
Primrose	978-0-330-51205-3	£3.99
Misty	978-0-330-51206-0	£3.99
Lulu	978-0-330-51207-7	£3.99
Poppy	978-0-330-51208-4	£3.99